The Colorful Adventures of Cody & Jay:

A Coloring and Activity Book

Goldest Karat Publishing
340 S Lemon Ave #1077
Walnut, CA 91789

For more Colorful Adventures books, visit us online at
www.goldestkarat.com

THIS BOOK BELONGS TO:

Jay

Cody

MY NAME IS:

_____

I AM _____ YEARS OLD.

MY FAVORITE COLOR IS

_____

I LOVE TO

_____

Cody and Jay love to go fishing but where are all of the fish? Draw what you think is in the water underneath their boat.

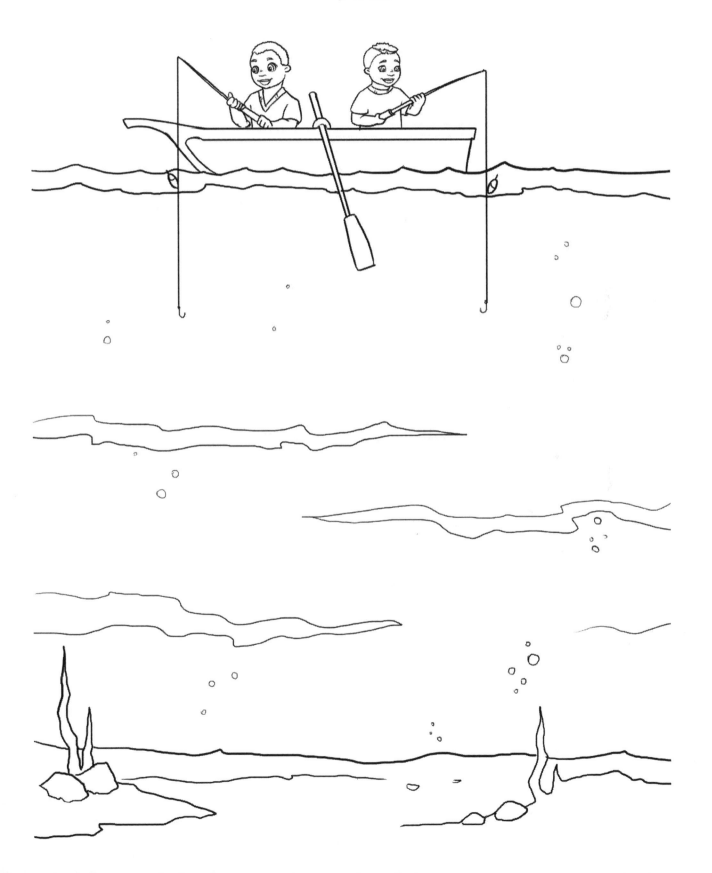

Look what Cody and Jay found in outer space!

Draw the rest of his alien family.

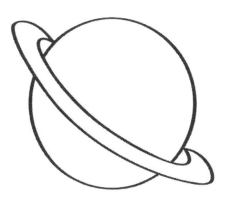

If you had a magic wand, what would you wish for?

_____

_____

_____

_____

Circle what you think Cody should wish for!

75 cupcakes   A trip to the beach

A new bicycle   A pet kangaroo

What three things make you REALLY happy? Write them in the star below!

Fill in the missing vowels to discover the hidden sentence!

TH_R_ _S _NLY _N_ M_,

_ W_LL B_ _LL TH_T _ C_N B_!

If you were a superhero, what superpower would you want to have? Why?

_____

_____

_____

_____

What would your superhero name be?

_____

_____

Jay is ready to drive his racecar but he needs your help adding a cool design!

Cody & Jay made $100 from washing cars, what do you think they should buy?

_____

_____

_____

What should they buy for a friend?

_____

_____

If you could fly anywhere in the world, where would you go?

_____

_____

Why?

_____

_____

_____

Add a cool design to Jay's skateboard.

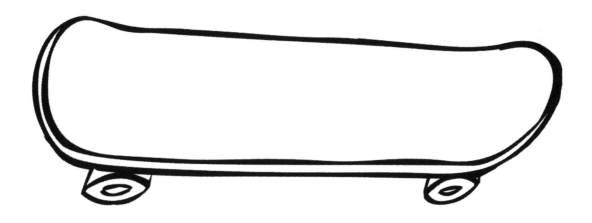

Design your own pirate flag.

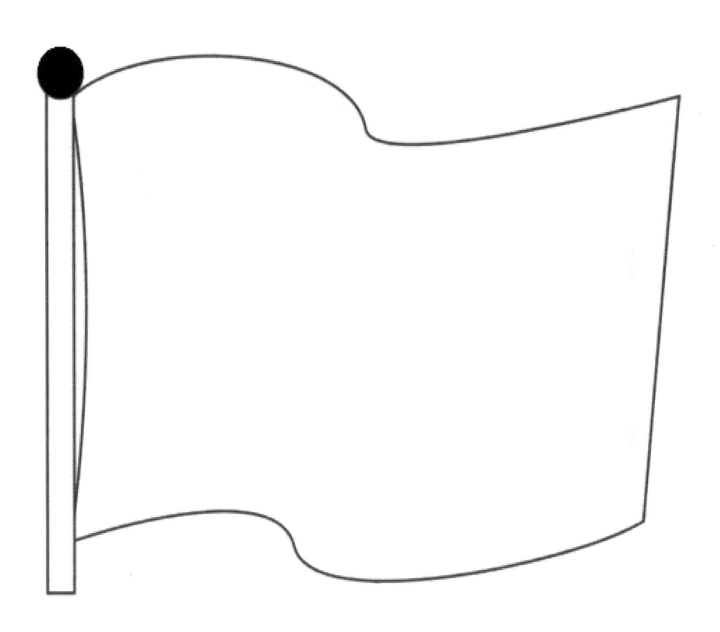

What do you want to be when you grow up?

_____

_____

_____

Why?

_____

_____

_____

_____

Fill in the missing letters A, T, I and O to discover the hidden sentence!

Y_U C_N
D_ _M_Z_NG
_H_NGS _F
Y_U TRY

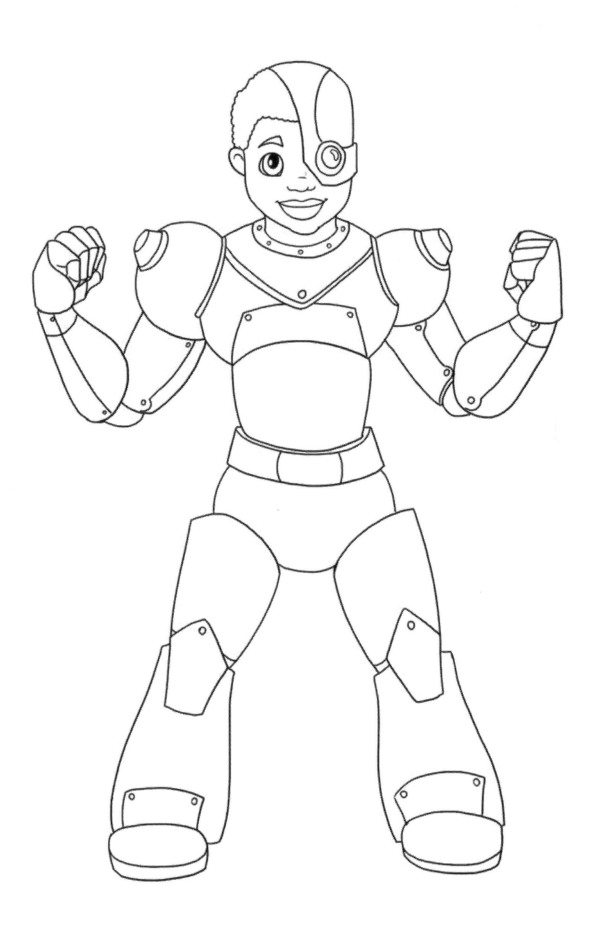

Jay loves to read! Use your imagination to finish writing the story:

Once upon a time there was a little boy who found a magic whistle. Every time he blew the whistle,

_____

_____

_____

_____

_____

_____

Oh No! The zebra has lost its stripes! Help draw him some new ones!

Circle some of your favorite things to eat!

What is your favorite sport? Design the helmet below.

THE END

41377586R00028

Made in the USA
San Bernardino, CA
10 November 2016